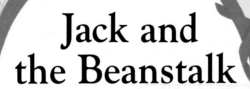

Jack and the Beanstalk

❧ Fairy Tale

Adapted
Jane Jerrard

Illustrated by
Susan Spellman

Publications International, Ltd.

Long ago, there lived a poor woman and her son, Jack. They had no money and no food, so the woman decided Jack must take their cow into town and sell it.

On the road into town, Jack met a strange old man who asked to buy the cow. The man offered Jack five magic beans for her, and Jack agreed, thinking that it was quite a bargain!

When Jack told his mother about the good trade he had made, she said, "You foolish boy! Now we must go hungry!" and threw the beans out the window.

The next morning, Jack awoke to find a giant beanstalk growing where the beans had fallen. It was so tall it grew to the sky! Jack climbed right up the beanstalk until he reached the clouds. There before him he saw a huge castle.

Jack walked up to the castle door. There stood the biggest woman he had ever seen! Jack asked if he could come in. The woman warned him that her husband, who was also a giant, would eat Jack. But Jack asked so nicely that the woman took him in and fed him breakfast.

As Jack finished eating, he heard the Giant coming. Quick as a wink, the woman popped Jack into the unlit oven, safely out of sight.

The Giant roared,

> "Fe fi fo fum,
> I smell the blood
>   of an Englishman!
> Be he live or be he dead,
> I'll grind his bones
>   to make my bread!"

"It is only the stew," said his wife.
After the Giant had eaten, he called
for his gold. The Giant counted his
coins until he fell asleep. Jack
grabbed one of the bags of gold.
Then he ran as fast as he could to
the beanstalk and climbed down.

His mother was happy to have him home, and the gold bought them food. But as soon as the coins were spent, Jack again climbed the beanstalk and asked the Giant's wife to let him into the castle.

The woman did not want to let him in. She did not recognize Jack and told him that the last boy she fed had stolen her husband's gold. But Jack asked so nicely for a drink that she took him in and gave him some water.

Jack had just finished when he heard the Giant coming, so he ran to hide in the oven.

> "Fe fi fo fum,
> I smell the blood
>   of an Englishman!
> Be he live or be he dead,
> I'll grind his bones
>   to make my bread!"

His wife said, "It is the soup you smell." After the Giant had eaten, he called for his hen that laid golden eggs. Soon the Giant fell asleep. Jack grabbed the magic hen and hurried home.

Each day the hen laid a golden egg, and Jack's mother was very happy. But Jack still longed for adventure. So he climbed up the beanstalk again and tiptoed into the castle. There, he hid behind a broom.

Soon the Giant and his wife came in. The Giant looked around and bellowed, "Fe fi fo fum, I ..."

His wife ran to look in the oven, but no one was there.

The Giant sat down at the table and called for his wife to bring him his magic harp. Jack watched as a lovely golden harp was set before the Giant.

When the Giant roared, "Sing!" the harp played a beautiful song all by itself and sang along in a soft voice. The music quickly put the Giant to sleep. Jack crept from his hiding place behind the broom and grabbed the harp.

"Help, Master!" called the magic harp, waking the Giant. He leaped up with a roar of rage and grabbed at Jack.

Jack ran faster than he had ever run before. He ran straight to the beanstalk and slid all the way down to the ground. Then Jack grabbed his ax and, with one blow, chopped down the beanstalk. Down it crashed, and with it crashed the Giant. That was the end of the magic beanstalk—and the Giant!